Boy versus Fly

A Dean Bean Adventure

Written and Illustrated by
Daniel Beitchman

To All the Boys & Girls,
Watch out for those
pesky flies!

Boy Versus Fly
A DEAN BEAN ADVENTURE

ISBN: 978-1-7751796-2-7 (sc)
ISBN: 978-1-7751796-1-0 (ebook)

DANCO CREATIVE

Dedicated to Mom and Dad Bean

"He shoots—he misses!" shouted Weston.

"More like missed again," Terry said. "Dean Bean, if you want to score a goal, you're going to need some new moves to get one past me."

"I know, Terry. I'm not giving up. I will score a goal on you one of these days," Dean Bean said, wondering how he would do it.

Dean Bean then felt his phone buzz. "Time for me to go home for dinner now. See you at school tomorrow," Dean Bean said to Weston and Terry.

Dean Bean walked home thinking about ball hockey. *I am going to learn a slap shot, and it will be so fast I will score for sure.* Terry won't see it coming.

As he walked, his thoughts slipped away from hockey. "I'm hungry," Dean Bean said to himself.

As Dean Bean turned the corner, he could see his dad out walking Oscar the dog. Dean Bean caught up to his dad and, after an excited greeting from Oscar, told his dad about his plan to learn a slap shot.

"The slap shot is an important part of the game, Dean, and like I have told you many times, practice makes perfect. Keep going, and someday you will get a shot past Terry. I promise."

Dean Bean told his dad how hungry he was and asked his dad if they were having meatloaf for dinner. "Tonight we're having tofu lasagna, kale salad with nuts and raisins, and sweet potato ice cream for dessert," Dad Bean explained.

"Oh," he responded with disappointment. "Dad, I was hoping we would have meatloaf tonight. You know I played ball hockey all day, and meatloaf is good for athletes," Dean Bean said.

"Meatloaf is a wonderful idea. Next Sunday we will make vegan meatloaf with feta, walnut, and grape salad for dinner. Your mother and brother will love it too," Dad said.

"Oh, ah, I, ummmm, yuck," Dean Bean whispered to himself, not knowing what to say to his dad. Dean Bean already knew that he didn't like vegan meatloaf, even though he had never had it and didn't even know what it was.

When Dad and Dean Bean got home, they called Mom and Dean's brother, Thomas, to dinner.

As they were eating, something in the distance caught Dean Bean's attention. After looking around the room for a minute or two, Dean Bean announced, "There is a fly in the kitchen. It is really fast and buzzes loudly, and it zips around like a motorcycle in the air! Dad, does it do anything except fly around and buzz-buzz people?" Dean Bean asked.

"Dean, dear," said his mom, "don't concern yourself with the fly. Just eat your salad. Your father will take care of the fly."

Dad Bean focused his sights on the fly, and as it flew by the dinner table, like a flash of lightning, he reached into the air and caught the fly with his bare hand!

"Got ya!" Dad Bean said with confidence.

"Wow, Dad!" Dean Bean and his brother, Thomas, said at the exact same time.

"What just happened? How did you do that?" Dean Bean asked his dad.

Thomas said, "Wow, Dad!" again.

"I have super-fast reflexes, and I have a trick for catching flies. Your mother calls me Superfly because she thinks I am a superhero that can catch any fly, big or small, fast or slow," he said as the buzz of the fly was tickling his hand.

"I'm going to let this fly outside and wash my hands," said Dad Bean. "I will teach you my fly-catching trick if you eat half of your salad by the time I get back."

Neither Dean Bean nor Thomas ate any of the salad. They would have to learn how to catch a fly on their own.

The next day, while walking to school, Dean Bean and Thomas talked about how cool it was that their dad was Superfly and that he could catch a fly with his bare hands.

"I am going to catch flies just like Dad did," Dean Bean said to Thomas as they walked up the front steps of their school.

As they headed off to different classes, Dean Bean gave Thomas a high five and said, "Good luck with your grammar test, bro. See you at home!"

```
1 x 7 = 7
2 x 7 = 14
3 x 7 = 21
4 x 7 = 28
5 x 7 = 35
6 x 7 = 42
7 x 7 = 49
8 x 7 = 56
9 x 7 = 63
10 x 7 = 70
```

Later that morning in Ms. Anne's math class, Dean Bean noticed there was a fly in the classroom. It landed on Ms. Anne as she was writing on the board.

Ms. Anne didn't notice the fly. I need to put a stop to this, Dean Bean thought to himself. "I don't think the fly should be in the classroom. He will buzz-buzz, and we won't be able to learn any math. It's up to me to catch it."

Dean Bean watched the fly for a minute or two. As it flew beside him, Dean Bean got out of his desk and started to chase the fly around the classroom. He tried to grab it, and grabbed at it again, but he wasn't even close. The fly always saw him coming.

Ms. Anne was helping Johnny C. and didn't notice Dean Bean chasing the fly until he knocked over a box of popsicle sticks. That was when the whole class turned around to see what Dean Bean was doing now.

Ms. Anne asked Dean Bean what he was doing. Dean Bean told her he was trying to catch the fly in the classroom. "It landed on you before. It is buzz-buzzing and bugging the class."

"Dean, why don't you return to your desk? That fly is not bothering anyone," Ms. Anne said.

The whole class snickered, but Dean Bean wasn't listening. He was focused on the fly as he took off his right shoe with his left hand. "I'm going to get you, fly!" Dean Bean yelled out, throwing his shoe at the fly and toward the window!

CRASH!

"Dean, *no!*" said Ms. Anne, a little too late.

"Look what you've done now. It was not the fly. You disrupted my class and broke a window! And you can't throw a shoe. What were you thinking?" Ms. Anne said with genuine frustration.

Dean Bean looked around and saw everyone staring at him, "I'm sorry, Ms. Anne. I didn't mean to disturb the class or break the window. I know the way to Principal Spoon's office," Dean Bean said, walking toward the door.

Dean Bean gulped as he knocked on Principal Spoon's office door. Dean Bean had promised Principal Spoon that he wouldn't get in any more trouble.

Principal Spoon popped his head out of his office. "I heard a window broke. Is anyone hurt?" he asked Dean Bean.

"No, nobody got hurt, Principal Spoon."

"Thank goodness! I am relieved that no one got hurt. What happened, Dean? Did you break the window?"

"Yes, Principal Spoon. I was trying to catch a fly, and it kept getting away, so I threw my shoe at it. The window broke, and I lost my shoe."

"Wow, Dean, that was a bad idea."

"Are you mad at me, Principal Spoon?" Dean Bean asked.

"We are still friends, Dean, but my job is to run this school so that everyone can learn in a safe environment. I don't like that you threw a shoe and broke a window," Principal Spoon said. "I need to call your parents and discuss how you will pay for the broken window and get your just desserts. Did you apologize to Ms. Anne and the rest of the class?" Principal Spoon asked.

"Yes, I apologized to Ms. Anne and the class. I know that I messed up big this time. I'm really sorry for throwing the shoe and breaking the window. It's that fly. I didn't even come close to catching it. My dad caught a fly with his bare hand. I don't think I will ever do that."

"Dean, Dean. I don't have any more time for this. I'm going to send you home now. See you back at school tomorrow. You can wait in the office until your parents pick you up."

"I'm sorry, Principal Spoon. I'm glad that we are still friends. It was wrong to chase the fly during class. See you tomorrow."

Leaving Principal Spoon's office, Dean Bean asked himself "What kind of punishment comes with 'just desserts'?"

Later that night, Dean Bean's mom and dad wanted to talk with him about what had happened at school. They called Dean Bean to the kitchen for a family meeting.

"Dean, dear, we can't have you get in any more trouble at school. We thought you were doing so well. What happened today?" Mom Bean asked him.

"There was a fly in Ms. Anne's class, and I thought I could catch it just like you did, Dad. It didn't work, so I threw my shoe at it," Dean Bean explained. "I made a big mistake interrupting the class, throwing my shoe, and breaking the window. I'm really sorry I did that," Dean Bean said.

"It is very mature of you to admit your mistake and apologize. Your mother and I hope you learned from your mistake," Dad Bean said. "Now you have to repay us for the broken window. Since you don't have any money, we decided that you will have to do daily household chores for one month after school. You won't be able to go out to play with your friends until everything is done, including your homework."

Dean agreed and told them he had never done any chores before.

"We will teach you how to clean and do household chores," Mom Bean said.

"Thank you for not getting mad at me. I love you, Mom and Dad. I will do the best chores to pay you back."

As Dean Bean walked back upstairs to his room, he said to himself, "I'm going to catch that fly sooner or later."

Dean Bean had gotten really good at doing the chores; his mom and dad even told him so.

Then one day as he was dusting, he heard in the distance a familiar buzz-buzz-buzz. "Not you again, fly," Dean Bean said.

As it flew by, Dean Bean reached out to catch the fly; he missed. He continued with his chores, trying to ignore the fly and putting away the dishes in the dishwasher before getting out the vacuum.

Dean Bean started to vacuum when an idea came to him. "That's it!" he said to himself excitedly.

Dean Bean turned off the vacuum and waited.

A few moments later, the fly returned, and Dean Bean was ready. As if trained by ninjas, he switched on the vacuum and extended the hose in the air.

"Say goodbye, fly," Dean Bean said, waving the hose in front of the fly, hoping to catch it. He turned off the vacuum and put down the handle. The room was silent.

Dean Bean scanned the room looking for the fly. Not hearing its buzzing and not seeing it, he knew he had done it. "Got ya! You messed with the wrong kid this time!"

"Wow, Dean Bean," he said to himself. "It was a way better idea to vacuum the fly than to throw a shoe. Who would have thought I could learn so much from trying to catch a silly fly?"

As he put the vacuum back together and started cleaning again, out of the corner of his eye, he noticed something.

"Is that a spider?"

Daniel Beitchman lives in Toronto, Canada. He has a Bachelor's Degree in History from the University of Western Ontario in London, Ontario and studied art and design at George Brown College in Toronto. He is married and a step father, grandfather, brother and uncle.

Boy versus Fly, A Dean Bean Adventure: is the first published work by Daniel. It was inspired by some of his own experiences and love of finding humor in everyday life.

As for Dean Bean, he is ready for another adventure...

Visit www.danielbeitchman.com